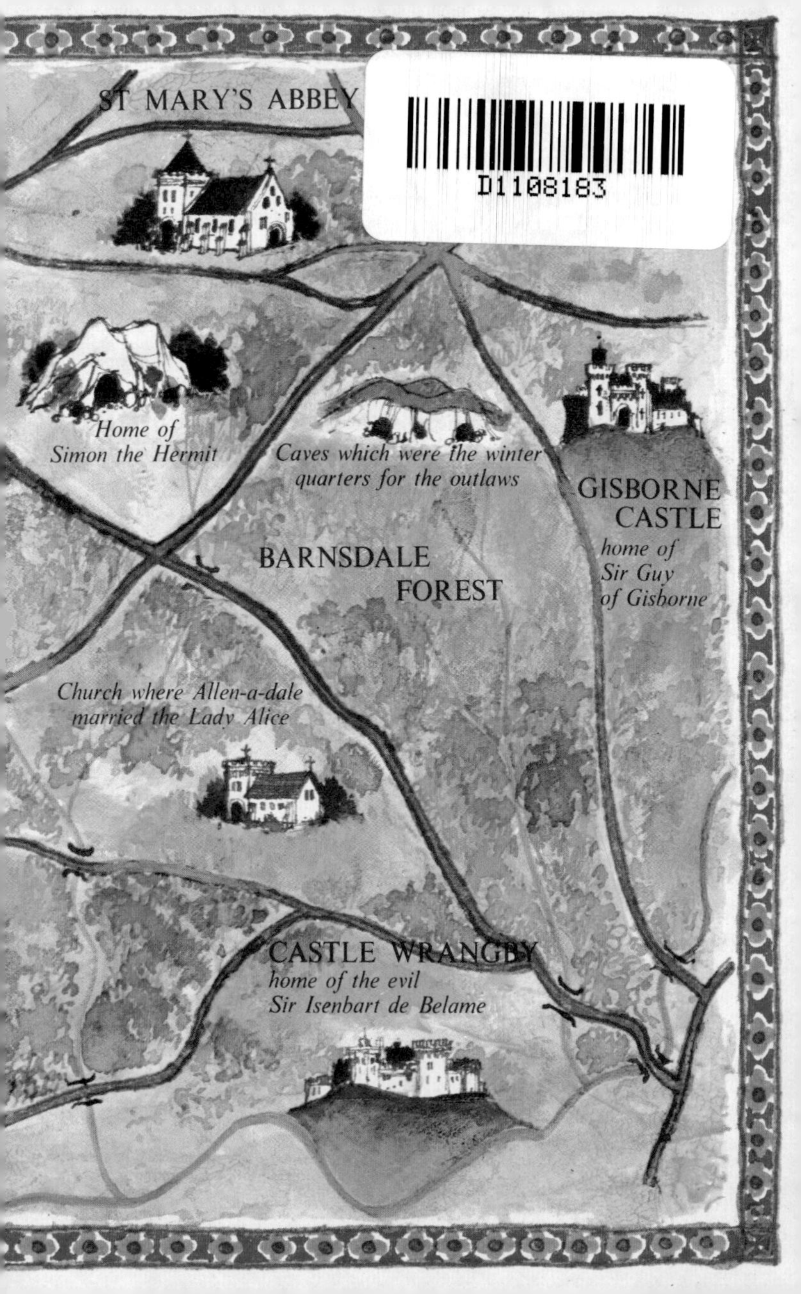

ST MARY'S ABBEY
D1108183
Home of
Simon the Hermit
Caves which were the winter
quarters for the outlaws
GISBORNE
CASTLE
home of
Sir Guy
of Gisborne
BARNSDALE
FOREST
Church where Allen-a-dale
married the Lady Alice
CASTLE WRANGBY
home of the evil
Sir Isenbart de Belame

*Harold, the last of the Saxon kings, died at Hastings in 1066. Duke William of Normandy, the Conqueror, became King of England. The knights and lords who had supported him were rewarded with the rich Saxon manors and estates. The Church had supported William and so the monasteries also became rich and powerful.*

*For many years England was ruled harshly, not only by William but by the Norman kings who came after him. The Saxon freemen as well as the* villeins *(peasants) hated the new laws and taxes and felt bitterly towards their Norman masters.*

*There were few books in those days. Most men could not read and so the tales they heard were sung and told to them by travelling minstrels.*

*The hero of many of these stories was Robin Hood. Some of the ballads which were sung about him can be read from old manuscripts though over the years the stories have been altered and added to by many writers.*

# ROBIN HOOD
## outlawed

by DESMOND DUNKERLEY

with illustrations by BERNARD BRETT

Ladybird Books Loughborough

## Robin becomes an outlaw

It was early morning in midsummer yet the day was already warm. Hardly a breeze stirred the leaves of the broad trees and the only sound was the hum of insects. Few men came this way save the king's foresters, keeping guard over the royal deer, for it was one of the loneliest parts of Sherwood Forest.

Yet the tall young man leaning against a tree was not a forester. His tunic and hose of green were those of a Saxon freeman, and the bow he held was not of the short Norman kind but a long Saxon one of yew, as tall as himself. He stood at the edge of a clearing in which three deer were grazing. But the young man was not looking at the deer. It was the bushes beyond them on the far side of the glade that he studied intently.

Suddenly the bushes moved slightly and an arrow sped from them straight to the nearest doe. The deer fell dead while the others dashed off in fright. Then all was still again. The watching man waited fully a minute before the bushes moved again. Then a man in the rough homespun tunic of a villein emerged stealthily from his hiding place. He looked warily about him before running to the deer he had killed.

Drawing a knife from his belt he quickly cut hunks of meat from the carcase, wrapped them in a piece of old cloth and stuffed them inside his tunic. Then, bending low, he scampered back to his hiding place.

The watching man drew in his breath. 'Oh, Will!' he whispered to himself. 'Will Scarlet, lad, what have you done? You'll lose a hand if you're caught with royal venison.' After a moment's thought he hurried off through the trees and came suddenly face to face with the villein, whose hand dropped instantly to the knife in his belt.

'Will,' said the man in green, 'what madness is this? Is there not food enough for you at my table?'

Will Scarlet recognised the speaker at once and gave a fierce laugh.

'Not that, Master Robin, for everyone knows there is enough to eat at Locksley Hall.'

'Then why?' asked Robin.

'It's for my sister,' said Scarlet. 'She lives on Guy of Gisborne's land and she is sick and cannot work. There the rule is that those who do not work may not eat. And so the sickness worsens and she may die.'

Robert of Locksley listened with pity and anger to Scarlet's tale, knowing too well the truth of it. Rich Norman landholders like Sir Guy of Gisborne treated their villeins little better than slaves.

They allowed them no rights and no possessions, and dealt out many cruel punishments. On the estate of Robert of Locksley however things were different. A freeman and landholder of proud Saxon blood, his villeins were treated and cared for well, holding their own strips of land and grazing their own animals.

For this he was hated by his Norman neighbours, who had many times tried to win his land by force or trickery. As long as the rent for the land was paid regularly to the Abbot of St Mary's to whom it belonged, and as long as he broke no laws, Robin knew that Locksley Hall was safe. His villeins, like Scarlet, could live there like men and not like serfs.

His thoughts were interrupted by the harsh cry of a jay high in the trees ahead. A second call came, harsher and more urgent than the first. Robin laid his bow and quiver of arrows at the foot of the great oak by which they stood. Taking Scarlet's arm, he said in a low voice, 'Place your bow and arrows and the meat from your tunic here beside mine. Quickly, man, and come with me,' he urged, as Scarlet hesitated. 'You will have them back later, never fear.' Will Scarlet did as he was told and followed Robin along the path. He looked back when he had gone a little way, and saw with amazement and fear that all their things had gone.

'Keep close behind me, Will,' said Robin's firm voice from ahead, and Scarlet followed, looking fearfully to right and left.

As they rounded a bend in the path, their way was blocked by two burly foresters.

'What brings a Saxon freeman and his serf this deep into the forest?' demanded the black-bearded leader of the two.

'A freeman, be he Norman or Saxon, may walk where he chooses,' replied Robin, meeting the other's rough stare. 'I chose my companion also, and would do again before I chose the company of a Norman like you.'

'I know you, Robert of Locksley, proud-tongued Saxon that you are,' said the forester angrily.

'And I know you, Black Ivo, for a cowardly Norman bully,' replied Robin sternly, 'and I will mark you when the time comes. Now, let us pass!' Pushing between the two foresters Robin continued along the path, followed by Will Scarlet.

At last the trees thinned out and they came to the edge of the common land which lay between forest and cultivated land.

'Why, look!' said Robin. 'There are the bows and arrows and your venison, Will.'

Scarlet saw their things lying by a bush. He was sure they had not been there a moment before. Shaking with fear, he turned to Robin.

'Master,' he said in a trembling voice, 'is this witchcraft, or the magic of wood spirits?'

'Neither, Will, but the work of friends of mine, as was the jay's warning call a while back.' Robin paused and then added, 'But you have nothing to fear from them, and maybe one day they will let

you meet them. Until then, say nothing. Now be on your way, and take care that none of Gisborne's men sees you hand the meat to your sister. And Will,' he called after Scarlet, 'when that is done, hurry back to Locksley Hall. Tell Stutely of the delay and that I'll return as soon as I've seen the Lady Marian safely back with her father.'

Robin picked up his bow and quiver and set off again into the forest. His steps were light and quick for he was on his way to meet the Lady Marian Fitzwalter whom he had known and loved since childhood. She had been visiting the castle of her uncle, Sir William de Beauforest, and now Robin was to escort her to her home at Malaset.

Robin made his way surely through the forest, for he knew every path and deertrack in Sherwood. When he had gone some distance he came out onto a main track which led from Nottingham to Barnsdale forest.

Stopping suddenly, he bent down beside a bare patch of ground. Robin studied a few broken twigs, seemingly there by chance.

'A mounted knight and ten men-at-arms,' he murmured to himself, 'halted on this road a mile to the south. What can this mean?' Robin feared that armed men in Sherwood meant trouble.

He crossed the bridleway and plunged deep into the forest again before swinging round and following a narrow path along the bank above the road. He stopped when he heard the jingle of harness ahead of him, and the soft whinny and snort of a horse. He crept forward slowly and parted the bushes slightly with his hand.

In the hollow below him, hidden from the path by thick undergrowth, sat a knight on horseback. Beside him stood five men-at-arms, and looking carefully Robin could just make out other shadowy figures on the far side of the track. Then Robin's face set grimly as he saw the mounted man's shield with its mailed fist emblem.

'Sir Roger de Mortmain!' muttered Robin, 'and in ambush. But for what poor soul, I wonder?' The question was answered by a man who came running through the trees and spoke to the knight.

'The lady approaches now, my lord, with her steward and only three other men on foot,' he said.

'Good,' replied the knight in a harsh Norman voice. 'You deal with the servants while I seize the lady's bridle.'

'Marian!' breathed Robin, for almost at once a small cavalcade had rounded the bend ahead.

The Lady Marian was talking quietly to her steward who rode beside her, while behind walked three villeins armed only with staves.

As the knight moved out onto the pathway Robin leapt between him and his prey.

'Hold, traitor knight!' he called, his bow levelled and fully drawn. The knight's horse reared and the men-at-arms halted in amazement. Then with a roar of rage the Norman rasped his sword from its scabbard.

'Locksley!' he bellowed, setting spurs to his mount. The horse had barely moved when there was a hum like that of a giant bee and de Mortmain fell from his saddle with a groan, a cloth-yard arrow through his throat. With a shout, the leader of the men-at-arms ran forward but fell dead at Robin's feet. The tiny arrow in his heart was no longer than a hand's span.

A wild cat's cry came from the bank above and smiling grimly, Robin glanced up in time to see a small shape flitting through the trees.

Realising that their foe was not alone but had wild friends they could not even see, the other soldiers set off back along the track with shouts of fear. More cries from high on either bank hurried them on their way. One soldier managed to scramble onto the dead knight's horse and gallop off.

Marian and Robin greeted each other tenderly, then Marian said anxiously, 'But now I fear for your life, Robin. The soldier who rode off heard your name and will soon have taken news of this to the dead knight's friends at Castle Wrangby.'

She thought for a moment and then shuddered. 'It is not called the "Evil Hold" for nothing, Robin. The men who live there, Belame, Gisborne and the others, are all as evil as de Mortmain was. Worse still, they are all friends of Prince John.'

'Don't fret, sweet lady,' Robin answered. 'As soon as I have seen you safely to your father's castle, I will return to Locksley Hall and see what must be done.' The sun was beginning to set as they hurried off through the forest.

When they reached Malaset, Sir Richard Fitzwalter echoed his daughter's warning. He was a noble knight, close to King Richard, and so had nothing to fear from either Gisborne or the lords of Castle Wrangby.

'But they will stop at nothing now where you are concerned,' he said grimly to Robin. 'By killing that base knight, richly though he deserved to die, your life and lands are forfeit, for you have put yourself outside the law – at least Prince John's law, if not King Richard's,' the knight added. 'All would be different if the Lion Heart were in England to deal justly with Norman and Saxon alike, but until he returns, guard yourself well at all times, for there is nothing I can do.'

'Keep safe the one I hold most dear in all the world,' replied Robin, 'then when the king returns and rights the wrongs that England suffers, I may beg your leave to make that duty my own.'

It was late evening and the sun had already set as Robin approached the cleared land surrounding Locksley Hall. He stopped on the edge of the forest aware of hidden danger. Although the air was warm after the heat of the day, there was no smell of wood-smoke from the cooking fires, nothing was moving and no evening birds sang.

Peering through the dusk, Robin could just make out the outline of the main Hall building. As he watched, several figures emerged, each carrying a blazing pinewood torch. The flames flickered and reflected on chain mail armour.

'Too late!' breathed Robin.

The torches clustered together for a moment. Then, as if at a given signal, all the torches curved into the air and dropped onto the roofs of the Hall and the surrounding cottages. Each roof became a blazing beacon, lighting up the sky.

Though taut with anger, Robin knew that he could do nothing until the flames had died down. Keeping in the shadows of the forest's edge he made his way round the clearing until he reached the side of the Hall which stood closest to the trees. There, clustered together in a dejected group, with their hands bound, sat Robin's steward, Scarlet, Will Stutely, Much the son of the miller and five more of his villeins. They appeared to be unguarded, which seemed unlikely, although Robin could see no soldier. The dry thatch had burnt fiercely, and the flames were dying. Robin knew that he would have to act quickly, for soon all the soldiers would return and his men would be led away.

Cupping his hands to his mouth, Robin gave the same jay's call that had been his warning earlier in the day. No one paid any attention except Scarlet whose head jerked up, looking this way and that.

'Good lad!' thought Robin. 'He has remembered!' Hearing the jay's call again, Scarlet stood up and stumbled over to the shadow of the stone porchway. He came out again pushed and buffeted by a single man-at-arms.

Both the drone of the arrow and the dying man's cry were lost in the crackle of the fire and the crash of falling timbers. Robin was at Scarlet's side almost before the soldier fell.

'Free the others – quickly now – and make for the forest!' Robin whispered urgently, giving Will the knife. He fitted another arrow to his bowstring, then knelt and waited. When the last of the freed men had vanished into the trees, he followed.

'Follow close and quickly, lads,' Robin said. 'We'll talk later.'

They halted at last, deep in the forest, by an oak tree in the middle of a wide glade. The villeins clustered round Robin in the bright moonlight.

'Listen to me carefully now,' said Robin, holding up his hand, 'and think well before you answer. Today, I killed Roger de Mortmain – an evil man, but a knight. Because of this, I am now outside the law and any may raise his hand against me. My lands are taken and my manor burned – I have no place now but the greenwood. But *you* can still go back, say that you ran in fear, and work your days for Guy of Gisborne to whom no doubt the Abbot of St Mary's will now rent the land.'

'No!' they cried. 'We'll come with you, Robin.'

Scarlet stepped forward. 'Will you lead us, master?' Robin nodded, and Scarlet spoke again. 'Those with families were taken away with the women and children,' he said. 'We have nothing here but the thought of day-long toil for an evil lord. What say you, lads?'

'Yes!' they shouted.

'Then each raise your hand,' called Scarlet, 'and swear to be true and loyal to our leader, Robert of Locksley!'

'No more of Locksley,' said Robin quietly, 'until King Richard makes it so.' He pulled the hood of his tunic over his head and led them, now outlaws all, deeper into Sherwood Forest.

### Robin meets Little John

Robin's voice rang clearly above the clamour of clashing swords and the shouts of struggling men. 'That's enough for today! Put up your swords.'

With groans of relief most of the dozen or so men dropped wearily to the grass and lay back where they fell, breathing heavily.

Scarlet and Much the miller's son however crossed to where Robin sat with his back against a fallen tree.

'This is harder than working in the fields, Robin,' said Scarlet, blowing out his breath.

'Aye,' said Robin with a smile, 'but your life could depend on how well you have learnt.'

It was a small glade in the heart of Sherwood Forest, far from the paths and tracks used by travellers. At one end a tiny stream flowed over pebbles, the sunlight of the hot summer day reflecting in the rippling water. Stutely and Dickon were cutting meat from a roasted buck and the hungry outlaws were beginning to move towards the fire.

Robin watched them. Since they had come to the greenwood and chosen him as their leader, he had driven them hard. They had been villeins then, slow of step and movement and unaccustomed to using a sword, quarterstaff or longbow. But Robin had known well that the lives of all of them depended on the skilful use of these weapons. Each day therefore had brought practice and more practice, and with it aching limbs and sore heads.

Now as he watched, Robin saw with pleasure a new lightness of step and keenness of eye in his men, that had come about in one month.

Standing up, Robin clapped a hand on Scarlet's shoulder.

'Come, Will – Much – let us eat. The sword play has made me hungry, and here is food fit for a king.'

'King Robin of Sherwood!' called Much gaily, and the other outlaws took up the shout.

'Nay, lads, I did not mean that,' said Robin quickly. 'There is only one king for England, and that is good King Richard.'

'They whisper in the market and the taverns,' put in Will Stutely, 'that Prince John holds all England for himself except Sherwood, and Robin Hood holds that for the king!'

'I am content with that,' said Robin, 'and with the name they have given me.'

When they had finished eating and the wooden plates had been scoured clean with sand and rinsed in the stream, Robin called his men round him.

'We have been outlaws now for four weeks,' he said. 'In that time you have learnt forest lore, and how to fight with sword and staff. Even the arrows you shoot, now usually hit the mark!'

The outlaws laughed, remembering some of their early efforts. 'But now the time has come,' Robin went on, 'to talk of rules by which our company must live. We have been made outlaws, and so to live we must rob. Many will journey through the forest who have grown fat and rich on money they have squeezed from the poor by too high rents and taxes, or unfair profit.'

'The Abbot of St Mary's,' muttered Scarlet.

'Yes,' said Robin, 'and many like him. All these we will stop, invite them to take food with us, and afterwards contribute to our treasury.'

This was greeted with a roar of laughter and approval.

'But some will pass through Sherwood,' Robin went on, 'whose goods we shall not touch and whom we shall not harm. Let any honest peasant or yeoman pass in peace. Let any knight or squire who is not proud, ride on. Many will come who may need our help. Those we will provide for from the goods and money that we take.' Again the outlaws agreed.

'One last thing,' said Robin quietly. 'I ask you not to harm any woman, no matter how proud or haughty.' He stood up. 'Now call in the two who guard the pathway, Will, that they may eat,' he said to Scarlet, 'and set two in their place. I will be back before nightfall.'

Robin picked up his bow and set off. Then he stopped at the edge of the clearing and held up his hunting horn.

'Should you ever hear three blasts of this,' he said, 'come quickly, for I shall need you.'

Robin made a wide, circular sweep of that part of the forest in which their camp was set. He did this each day, partly because he loved to be alone in the silence of the great trees, and partly to satisfy himself that no unwelcome visitors were coming too close.

After about an hour he came to a deep, fast flowing stream which he crossed by a narrow bridge made from a rough-hewn log. A little way into the trees on the other side he stopped suddenly and sniffed the air.

'Roasting venison?' Robin said. 'Now who can be cooking the king's deer so openly?' Following the smell, he came to a clearing in the trees.

On the far side a small fire crackled merrily. Suspended over the flames was a haunch of venison and Robin instantly recognised the man who sat beside the fire. A forester, with his back to a tree, was idly turning a skewer from which the meat hung. It was Black Ivo.

As Robin watched, there was a trampling in the undergrowth, and the tallest man that Robin had ever seen entered the glade. He was dressed in the rough homespun tunic of a peasant and carried a huge quarterstaff. Black Ivo looked up angrily.

'You lumbering ox,' he growled. 'Don't you know better than to blunder through the bushes like that? Don't you know you have no right to leave the road? Get you gone!'

'Your pardon, sir,' said the big stranger. 'I was

lost, so when my nose caught the scent of meat cooking, I made straight for the smell of it in the hope that some kind soul would give me supper and point me on my way.'

'You impudent rogue,' snarled Ivo. 'Be on your way before I knock some manners into your thick Saxon skull.' He got up and reached for his cudgel which leant against the tree, but before he could grasp it, the tip of the tall stranger's staff prodded him in the stomach. Ivo doubled up with a groan and the other end of the staff whirled round. It dealt him a blow on the back of the head which laid him unconscious on the ground.

Hidden by the bushes Robin chuckled silently as the huge man lifted the limp forester like a baby. He tied Ivo firmly to a tree and then sat down to demolish the forester's venison. As he ate he hummed or sang snatches of a ballad. Robin liked the gay, free air of him as much as he admired the tidy way he had dealt with the forester.

As the last piece of meat was disappearing, Ivo opened his eyes and looked around in a dazed fashion. Then he saw his dinner almost eaten.

'You scoundrel!' he roared. 'You shall pay for this. When I get free I'll break every bone in your hulking carcase.'

'Peace, man!' said the giant with a laugh. 'Think how much better it would have been for you if you had shared your meat with me in the first place. Now you have lost it all – and your temper too. So I'll be on my way and leave you to think about your lack of hospitality. No doubt your friends will pass by soon and set you free.' Followed by Black Ivo's shouts of rage, the big man went off into the trees.

Robin stepped into the glade and smiled down at Black Ivo. The forester looked up at him furiously. 'I suppose that great robber was one of your runaway rogues.'

'No, he wasn't,' replied Robin, 'but I hope to make him so within the hour.'

'Set me free!' raged Ivo. 'Untie me and I'll teach you both a lesson you won't forget.'

'Brave words from one who's just been given a lesson,' said Robin. 'Sit there awhile and think about your sins. You will be freed when you hear a jay's call at sunset.' Robin hurried off. He knew that the tall stranger would have to cross the narrow bridge, and Robin wanted to be there first. Since he knew every little track, Robin reached the stream first. He crossed the bridge and settled down to wait.

Bellowed snatches of song soon told him that Black Ivo's dinner companion approached. Robin cut a staff from a young sapling and waited until the tall man emerged from the trees and set foot on the bridge. Then he too started to cross. The two men stopped in the middle of the log and looked at each other.

'Step back!' said Robin. 'Did you not see that I was already on the bridge before you started to cross?'

The big fellow looked down at Robin and said with a smile, 'Get out of my way little man, before I tip you into the water!'

Robin was two inches taller than his six-foot bow yet he barely came up to the other's shoulders.

'Not so little that I cannot teach you some Sherwood manners,' he replied. 'Guard yourself!' With staff twirling Robin attacked his opponent furiously. The big man was amazed to find that Robin's strength was almost equal to his own. For some minutes they fought and at the same time had to keep their footing on the narrow bridge. Suddenly the big man aimed a left and right swing of his staff at Robin's head. Robin parried the blows but was unable to avoid the third, which flashed through his guard and swept him into the water.

The big man bent down. 'By the saints!' he said, peering into the stream, 'I hope I haven't drowned him for he was no mean fighter.'

'I am here,' called Robin, crawling onto the bank a little way downstream. 'You won, and now I do not need to cross the bridge.'

The giant joined Robin and they shook hands. 'I am glad you are not hurt. You fought as well as anyone I have met,' he said. Then, with a laugh, he asked, 'Now may I cross the bridge?'

'Aye,' replied Robin, laughing too, 'but where are you travelling to?'

'Here and there,' said the other. 'I am a serf who has run away from his lord and so can go nowhere – and anywhere.'

'That's a long way,' said Robin gravely, 'and you need supper first.' He raised the hunting horn to his lips and blew three loud, clear notes which echoed through the woods. They heard sounds of hurried movement in the distance and soon saw men running through the trees towards them. Will Scarlet was the first to arrive, followed by Will Stutely.

Soon Robin was surrounded by his men.

'What has happened to you, master?' asked Scarlet, looking at Robin's dripping figure. He glared at the stranger.

Robin told them of how Black Ivo was tricked out of his dinner, and of the fight on the bridge. Then he turned to the tall man. 'We are outlaws who, like you, could stand no more of evil Norman lords,' he said. 'The greenwood is our home and we eat well of the king's deer. What say you to joining us?'

'Yes, gladly!' cried the big man, seizing Robin's hand.

'Men call me Robin Hood,' said the outlaw leader.

'I have heard much of you!' exclaimed the other. 'Now I shall serve you even more gladly.'

'And what is your name?' inquired Robin.

'I am John of Mansfield,' said the tall man, and then gave a great laugh, 'but men call me John Little!' The outlaws laughed too.

'We must re-christen him!' called Scarlet. 'Lay hold men!' All the outlaws seized John, who was helpless against so many. 'In with him!' cried Scarlet. The huge figure was swung into the water with a mighty splash.

'John Little you were,' said Scarlet solemnly as the new outlaw clambered out dripping wet and spluttering with laughter, 'but now I name you Little John!'

Later, round a blazing fire, dry and well fed, the outlaws listened as Little John told them of his adventures before meeting Black Ivo. When he mentioned the forester, Little John stopped his story and slapped his leg. 'I had forgotten the surly rogue I left tied up,' he said. 'I wonder if he is free yet?'

'Aye, he is,' said Robin. 'I told him he would be cut loose at the first jay's call after sunset.'

'Did you go back and free him then, master?' asked a puzzled Little John.

'No, not I,' replied Robin, 'but I have other friends in the forest whom one day you will meet when the time is right.'

With a hand to his mouth Robin gave the screech of a hunting owl, and only Will Scarlet seemed unamazed when an answering call came from the darkness of the trees around them.

**Robin meets Friar Tuck**

Summer had turned to autumn, and the leaves of the great beeches and oaks of Sherwood were beginning to change to brown and gold. Leaving the woodland glades which had been their summer home, Robin Hood and his band had made their winter quarters in warm dry caves to the north of Nottingham. Here the forest was full of rough hills and craggy rocks.

Their Lincoln green tunics and hose, too, had been changed for clothes of russet brown so that they could pass through the forest unseen by all but the keenest eyes. Many days were wet and cold when only the scouts were out guarding the narrow, hidden pathways to their hideout. Even the main tracks became deep in mud and the only travellers passing through the forest were beggars, pedlars and pilgrims whose only home was the open air.

One of these hardy wayfarers, a pilgrim, was sitting by a blazing fire in the main cave. As payment for a dry bed and a hearty breakfast, he was telling the outlaws of his travels.

'And did you really see King Richard himself?' asked Much the miller's son.

'I did,' replied the brown-faced traveller, 'and stood as close to him as I am to you.'

The outlaws, simple villeins to whom the king was a distant and remote figure, found it wonderful to be listening to a man who had actually seen him.

'And what is more,' the pilgrim went on, 'I heard the Lion Heart speak.'

The outlaws gasped in amazement and no one spoke until Robin said, 'And what did the king say? Did he speak of England and of coming home?'

'One question at a time,' the pilgrim answered gently. 'Yes, he spoke of England, and with longing, too, I thought. But no, he did not speak of coming home. His mind is set on winning back Jerusalem from the Turks and nothing else. He'll not be home till that is done.'

'But does he not know how ill the land is

governed?' asked Robin with a hint of anger and impatience in his voice. 'Does the king not know that his brother Prince John, and those false lords about him, grow rich and fat by cruel taxes and unjust laws?'

'He knows,' sighed the pilgrim. 'Every ship that comes from England brings some new reminder of it, and yet he stays – and puts his hopes on men like you.'

'Like us?' said Robin in surprise. 'How so?'

'I was beside the king,' the traveller said, 'when a despatch came to him. Reading it, the Lion Heart said, "There must be freeborn men in England still who will not stand for these injustices, or I am king of nothing worth the name!"'

The pilgrim looked at Robin. 'You are the Robin Hood, are you not, whose deeds I hear about in every place between here and the sea?' Robin nodded. 'Then if the stories of these deeds are true,' the pilgrim said, 'it was of you, and men like you, that good King Richard spoke. Enough of serious talk! Here is one more tale before I go. It concerns a monk, no less, whom you would do well to seek to join your band. He is a warlike fellow if ever I met one.'

'A monk?' cried Little John in surprise. 'A warlike friar? Now there's a man I'd like to meet!' The giant outlaw gave a huge laugh. The only monks they had ever met, apart from their elderly village priests, had been the Abbot of St Mary's and his followers. That monastery, like many others in England, owned much land, and the abbot and his monks grew fat on the hard work of others. For warlike duties they kept men-at-arms like the ones who had burnt Locksley Hall.

'When you do meet him,' said the pilgrim, 'go carefully! He is no ordinary churchman.'

Robin's interest was aroused. When he had first brought his men to Sherwood there had been twelve of them. There were other outlaws living in the forest, but many of these had been cut-throats and evil men who robbed rich and poor alike. Robin had shown them no mercy. Others had been simple serfs like his own men, driven to the greenwood by cruel masters. These had been glad to join Robin Hood, whose fame had become known to all. Many of the newcomers knew other Saxons who waited for their chance to do the same. These Robin had sought out and asked them to become his comrades in the forest, and now his band numbered thirty.

Such a one was George-a-Green, the pound-keeper of Wakefield, with whom Robin had fought for a whole day. In the same way Robin had fought Little John's cousin, Arthur-a-Bland of Nottingham, a famous man with the quarterstaff, and won him to their company. Both now sat listening as the pilgrim told his tale.

'I was at Copmanhurst in Fountain Dale,' the pilgrim said, 'and met Friar Tuck, as he is called, when I was tired and hungry. He fed me well, on royal venison, for he cares nothing for foresters. As we sat and talked, ten of the sheriff's men-at-arms and two of the foresters came by. Seeing the carcase outside, they hammered on the door, thinking they would take the friar prisoner for killing royal deer.'

'What did he do?' asked Little John eagerly.

'Tuck drove them off with his great staff,' the pilgrim said, 'and not one of the twelve escaped without an aching head or battered ribs!'

'One against twelve was nobly done,' said Little John admiringly.

'As they limped off by ones and twos as best they could,' the pilgrim added, 'the friar whistled up his dogs to speed them on their way.'

'Nobly done, indeed,' said Robin. 'Can you tell more of this Friar Tuck?'

'I know no more,' the pilgrim replied, 'except that when he came back from driving off the soldiers he was laughing loudly, as though he had enjoyed the fight, and saying that the exercise had done him good.'

'I like this holy man more and more!' cried Little John.

'I know Friar Tuck,' said a young outlaw who had joined the band a week before. He flushed now as all eyes turned towards him.

'Speak up then, Hal,' said Robin kindly, 'and tell us what you know.'

'Well,' said Hal, 'they say he was put out of Gray Friars Abbey because he caught fish from the Abbot's own fish pond to cook and eat in secret when the monastery food did not fill him up. When he was found out and the Abbot sought to punish him with bread and water, Friar Tuck threw the Abbot into the pond, and three of the brothers with him.'

The outlaws all laughed loud and long at this and the pilgrim said, 'The tale is true because the friar told me of it himself.'

'I know him for a good man, too,' Hal went on. 'My village was near to Copmanhurst, and often Friar Tuck would come with food and remedies for the old and sick folk. The day that I was beaten till I could not stand, the friar took me to his hut and cared for me. He hid me from the lord's soldiers when they came searching. When they had gone, he told me to go to Robin Hood in Sherwood and be his man.'

'He knew of me then?' asked Robin.

'Indeed master, and often spoke of you,' replied Hal.

'Then I must seek him out,' said Robin, 'for he sounds a fine comrade to have with us here in the forest.'

Telling Little John to follow with a dozen men within the hour, Robin set out at once. The rain had stopped, the clouds had cleared, and the forest smelt sweet and fresh in the watery sunlight. Robin travelled swiftly until, by about midday, he reached a broad stream.

Continuing along its course he came to a place where the trees opened out and the bank of the stream sloped gently down to the water. A small hut built of logs stood by the water's edge and sitting with his back against it, apparently asleep, was a broad and sturdy figure in monk's robes.

Laying down his bow and quiver, Robin drew out his long dagger and approached silently. Then with the tip of the blade at the friar's throat he said, 'Wake up, holy man, for I need to cross the stream. I do not wish to wet my feet so you will have to carry me across.'

The big figure opened his eyes slowly and looked up at Robin with a steady gaze.

'Up, lazy one,' cried Robin, 'up, and take me across or it will be the worse for you.'

Without a word the monk rose, bent his back onto which Robin climbed and was carried across the stream. As the monk stepped up onto the opposite bank Robin prepared to clamber off, but to his surprise was flung suddenly over the monk's head. He landed with a crash on his back and his dagger dropped from his hand. Before he could get to his feet, the friar's knee was in his ribs and two great hands were gripping his throat.

'Now, my fine fellow, you shall carry me back again,' said Friar Tuck. Slowly Robin waded back across the water, staggering under the weight of his burden. Any notion of tipping his rider into the stream left him, because of the pressure of the friar's hands about his neck.

As he reached the bank, Friar Tuck slid to the ground with a laugh. Before Robin could make for his bow, the shrill cry of some hunted animal came from the trees. The call was repeated again, more urgent than before.

'Arm yourself, friar!' cried Robin, notching an arrow to his bow.

'Against what foe?' the friar asked.

'Look yonder,' replied Robin. 'Now is the time to show the truth of all the tales of fighting skill that I have heard of you.'

Out of the trees to their left, a dozen men-at-arms came shouting.

'Fair odds!' roared Friar Tuck. He came out of his hut with a sword and buckler. ''Tis only a dozen of the sheriff's rascals.'

'The odds lengthen,' said Robin grimly. He pointed downstream to where twelve or more foresters, led by Black Ivo, were pouring from the trees towards them with swords levelled. Even as he spoke Robin loosed his first arrow at the leading soldier who pitched forward with the shaft through his heart. Two more long arrows followed the first, and two more soldiers fell.

As the rest halted uncertainly, Robin quickly put his horn to his lips and blew three long blasts. He knew that Little John and the outlaws with him could not now be far away. Then, loosing two more quick arrows in the other direction at the

advancing foresters, he dropped his bow and drew his sword from its scabbard.

'Back to back, Tuck!' he cried, 'and fight hard for a while. Help is on the way.'

'Aye, and more to come,' said the friar and putting two fingers in his mouth gave a shrill, piercing whistle. He had scarcely done this before he and Robin were surrounded by the foresters and men-at-arms who had joined forces. Robin fought furiously but silently, his sword whistling in a glittering circle of steel about him.

Behind him, with his broad back to Robin's, Friar Tuck fought as fiercely but with taunting roars and huge bellows of laughter.

Suddenly, with a great barking and baying, ten huge grey hounds leapt at the foresters from behind. They turned in fear to fight this new and terrible enemy as best they could. Black Ivo tried to rally them but although they were greater in number, the sheriff's men were now hard-pressed as Robin Hood and Friar Tuck took their chance to turn from defence to attack.

Above the cries of fighting men and the deep snarling of the dogs, there came a great shout from upstream.

Running from the trees came the outlaws, led by Little John.

'Away! Save yourselves!' cried Black Ivo, and his men scattered wildly into the cover of the forest, hastened on their way by a flight of arrows from Little John's band and by the snapping hounds at their heels.

Robin Hood and Friar Tuck leant wearily against the wall of the hut as the outlaws streamed past in pursuit.

'We'll see them safely clear of Copmanhurst,' called Little John as he ran by. Robin raised a hand in acknowledgment, then turned to Friar Tuck, who had found breath enough to whistle back his dogs.

'The stories I heard of you are true, good friar,' he said breathlessly.

'And I of you, Robin,' gasped the friar.

'You know me then?' asked Robin in surprise.

'I knew you were Robin Hood from the moment I woke with your knife point at my throat,' replied Friar Tuck with a laugh.

'Tell me, then,' said Robin, looking at him steadily, 'do you like the solitary life you lead?'

'I have liked it well enough,' answered the friar, 'until now.'

'And now?' asked Robin.

'Now I have a sudden longing for company,' laughed Friar Tuck. 'The kind of company that I might find in the greenwood with men whose hearts are free, led by one whom I have long admired.' He paused and stretched out his hand. 'Will you enrol me in your band, Robin?'

'With all my heart,' replied the outlaw leader warmly, and gripped the other's hand in his.

So Friar Tuck came to Sherwood Forest and for as long as they lived there, he was second only to Little John among the outlaw band of Robin Hood.

SHERWOOD FOREST
This picture has been based on a map of Nottingham and the Sherwood forest area. It shows where some of the events in the stories may have taken place and where some of the places mentioned in the books might have been situated.
LOCKSLEY HAL
where Robin live
before it was burn
down and he beca
an outlaw
COPMANHU
Robin Hood me
Friar Tuck
Log over the strea
where Little John
fought Robin Hoo
OUTWOODS HUNTING LODGE
Mounds which were th
home of Tull and Caw
Main summer quarters for
Robin Hood and his men
NOTTINGHAM CASTLE
home of the Sheriff
of Nottingham
to ASHBY